Enchanted Hearts™ series
In Friendship's Garden

ndship.

'Iinton

Illustration by Mary Maguire

Copyright© 1996
Lighten Up Enterprises
5223 Edina Industrial Blvd.
Edina, MN 55439-2910

Kindness is the sweet fragrance
in friendship's garden.

All people smile
in the same language.

Get down on your knees
and thank God
you are on your feet.

My world is better
having a friend like you,
who finds the good in everything,
and then gives it away.

Be of good cheer.
This counsel is of heaven.
—— Homer

Some days, our friendship is the only glue that holds me together.

God's favorite word is — come!
— Robert L. Sterner

You are the light of the world,
but the switch must be turned on.

A light heart lives long.
— *Shakespeare*

Take three deep breaths
— First!

We only look older, you and I.
Inside we're younger than ever.

Let's be grateful today for all the parts of us that do work!

The light within you is shining.
I'm honored to be your friend.

What a relief that I don't have to change others, only myself.

There ain't much fun in medicine, but there's a good deal of medicine in fun. —— Josh Billings

A smile takes but a moment, but its effects sometimes last forever.

— J.E. Smith

The most valuable gift you give me,
dear friend, is your goodness.

Laugh at yourself first,
before anyone else can.
— Elsa Maxwell

Normal day, let me be aware
of the treasure you are.

Life's blessings are placed within our reach, but not in our hands. Let's move forward and grab hold of all the good that is there.

Patience is the ability to count down
when you want to blast off.

It's so much easier to be negative.
Let's fool them all and
see the bright side.

So, we're getting older.
We won't stop laughing, will we?

Love your neighbor,
but don't pull down the hedge.
—— Swiss proverb

For just one hour today let's put busyness on the shelf and just BE.

Remember the little forgotten things
that bring a smile.

Praise does wonders
for our sense of hearing.
— Arnold Glasow

To get the full value of joy,
you must have somebody
to divide it with. —— Twain

*Those who bring sunshine to others
cannot keep it from themselves.*
—— James Barrie

Keep your face to the sunshine
and you will not see the shadows.
—— Helen Keller

Make the most of the best
and the least of the worst.
— Robert Lewis Stevenson

We never know when we will
be made wiser even by
the people we don't agree with.
—— Dorothy Larsen

If you can't see the bright side,
polish up the dark side.

*Too much of a good thing
can be wonderful.* — Mae West

The day most wholly lost is the one
in which one does not laugh.
—— Nicholas Chamfort

A friend is one who comes in
when the rest of the world
has gone out.

The shortest way to God is to bring comfort to the soul of your neighbor.

—— Aby Said

It is so easy to believe the best about you, my friend.

May we learn to enjoy
the little things — since
there are so many of them.

Happiness must be practiced — like playing the piano.

The greatest reward in friendship
is the satisfaction found
in your own heart.

Friendship is two clocks
keeping perfect time.

My spirit is renewed just thinking of the fun we share.

My own journey will be brighter
when I hold a candle to light the
path of a friend.

Laughter is the sunshine
of the soul.

Every good thought you're thinking is contributing to the rest of your life.

In friendship's garden may we sow courtesy, plant kindness and gather love.